Goodbye
Mog

Judith Kerr

Collins

An imprint of HarperCollinsPublishers

For Gail Penston
with love and thanks

First published in Great Britain by HarperCollins Publishers Ltd in 2002

5 7 9 10 8 6 4
ISBN: 0-00-714968-9

The HarperCollins website address is: www.fireandwater.com

Printed and bound in Belgium

Mog was tired. She was dead tired.
Her head was dead tired.
Her paws were dead tired.
Even her tail was dead tired.
Mog thought, "I want to sleep for ever."
And so she did.
But a little bit of her stayed awake
to see what would happen next.

What happened next was that everybody wept.
"Oh, why did Mog have to die?" wept Debbie.
"She was so lovely," wept Nicky.
"Well, she was quite old," said Mrs Thomas. Then she wept too.
Even Mr Thomas wept. He said, "She was our family pet.
We'll all miss her."

"Well, of course they'll miss me," thought Mog.
"They'll never manage without me.
But it's quite true – I *was* very lovely."

After this nothing happened for some time.
Debbie and Nicky talked about her.
"Remember how she used to hang her tail
in front of the telly?" said Nicky.
"Like this, you mean?" thought Mog.
But the telly shone right through her.

"She used to come into our beds," said Debbie.
"And look! Here I am!" thought Mog.
But nobody looked.
Mog thought, "They can't see me."

Then, suddenly one day there was a kitten in the house.
Mrs Thomas said, "Its mother couldn't look after it,
so I said we would. It will be our new family pet."
Mog thought, "This kitten is very small."
Mr Thomas said, "Are you sure it's big enough?"

The kitten was frightened of everything.
It was frightened of noise.

It was frightened of newspapers.

It was frightened of bags,

and it was very frightened of being picked up.

"Oh dear," said Mrs Thomas.
"It's not much of a pet, is it?" said Mr Thomas.
Mog thought, "This is the wrong sort of kitten."

"Just give it some peace," said Mrs Thomas.
"And play something quiet while I go to the shops."

"The kitten's had lots of peace now," said Nicky.
"It must be getting bored."

"Perhaps it would like some milk," said Debbie.

"Well, really!"
thought Mog,
"And in my
dish, too!"

"Look!" shouted Nicky. "Look where the kitten is!" It was a noisy shout.

The kitten was frightened of noise.

And newspapers and bags.
"Where's it got to?" shouted Mr Thomas.

"It's getting out!" shouted Mrs Thomas.
"Catch it quick!" shouted Nicky.
Mog thought, "This kitten is very stupid."

The kitten was not in the garden.

And not in the street.
"Suppose we never find it," said Nicky.
"It'll be all alone," said Debbie.

"I knew it," thought Mog.
"I knew they'd never manage without me.
They've got themselves the wrong sort of
stupid kitten and now they've lost it.
I'm going in."

She thought, "That kitten may be anywhere.
Who knows what's happening to it now."
Suddenly she heard a noise.
It was a kitten noise.

"Really," thought Mog.
"It never went out at all. Now what?"

The kitten looked at Mog.
The kitten crept up to Mog.
The kitten purred.
"Well I never," thought Mog.
"I believe this kitten can see me.
Perhaps it's not so stupid
after all."

Mog did a little jump.
The kitten jumped too.

She washed
her paw.
The kitten
washed its
paw too.

Mog hid under the newspapers. The kitten looked at Mog. Mog smiled.

The kitten hid too.

The kitten liked playing with the newspapers. Mog thought, "This kitten is not the wrong sort of kitten at all. It just needs a bit of help."

Then one of the bags fell over. All sorts of things fell out.

Mog and the kitten played with them.

Then they played with the bags.

Suddenly there was a bang. It was the bang of a door.

"Whatever has happened here?" said Mr Thomas.
"Perhaps we've had burglars," said Mrs Thomas.
Nicky said, "Why is that newspaper moving?"

"It's the kitten!" shouted Debbie.
"Don't touch it!" shouted Mrs Thomas.
"It'll scratch you!" shouted Mr Thomas.

"Perhaps it won't this time," said Debbie. "Come on, Kitty!"
The kitten looked at her. It didn't move.
"I only want to stroke you," said Debbie.
The kitten still didn't move.
Mog thought, "This kitten needs a bit of help."

She gave the kitten
a bit of help.

The kitten flew
through the air.
It was very surprised.

"Look," said Debbie. "The kitten likes me."
She stroked it. The kitten found it liked being stroked.

And it liked being tickled.

And it loved to play.
"I knew it," thought Mog. "I knew
this kitten only needed a bit of help."
"It's made quite a rumpus," said Mrs Thomas.

"That could be its name," said Nicky.
"We could call it Rumpus."
"Come on then, Rumpus," said Mrs Thomas.
"Let's get you something nice to eat."

"Well, we've really got our new family pet at last," said Mr Thomas.

Debbie said, "But I'll always remember Mog."

"So I should hope," thought Mog.
And she flew up and up and up and up right into the sun.